The Boy Who Dreamed DRAGONS

CARYL LEWIS ★ CARMEN SALDAÑA

PUFFIN

Albie was just like any other boy,
except for one thing . . .

Albie LOVED going to bed.

In Albie's house there
was no sudden need
for a drink of milk,

or for doing handstands
on the landing instead of
brushing teeth.

Albie just went straight to
bed, because at night . . .

Albie dreamed DRAGONS.

He dreamed all kinds of dragons –
some jewel-bright and fierce,
some softly scaled and whispery –
but whichever kind they were,
they stayed with him throughout
the night and the next day too.

There were **FIRE DRAGONS**, which were very handy
for browning toast for breakfast . . .

and **WATER DRAGONS** that came with Albie
when Mum took him swimming.

There were TREE DRAGONS too that showered him
with leaves when they went on walks in the woods.

In winter, there would be SNOW DRAGONS
that laid down icy paths so that Albie
could slide to school . . .

and CANDLE DRAGONS,
who lit up the lamp posts
on his way home.

Albie loved his dragons very much and his mum did too –
it was just that sometimes she worried about him.

"Are you sure you don't want to have any friends,
I mean, 'non-dragon' friends, over to play?"
she asked him one night, as he sat reading
by the fire with a WORD DRAGON
curled up in his lap.

Albie thought about it for a bit. He thought about how he always played with his dragons, while the other children played together, and how sometimes his eyes would be drawn to them and their laughter.

He shook his head. "It's OK – really it is."

So Mum gave him a soft smile and went to fetch hot chocolate.

That night, Albie dreamed
a new kind of dragon,
a lovely FRIEND DRAGON,
soft and quiet with beautiful
full-feathered wings.

Albie was sitting with it the next morning,
when the **FRIEND DRAGON** nudged him
with his nose . . .

Albie took a deep breath.
"OK," he said. "I'll ask if we can play."

Albie had just finished introducing his dragon
when one of the children LAUGHED.
Albie felt his face flush.

They couldn't see a dragon!

Albie tried to explain to them exactly where the dragon was,
but his mouth became dry and he ran out of words . . .
They said he should forget his silly dragon and
play ball with them instead.

Albie could feel his dragon's breath warm on the back of his neck
and knew that he could never pretend that his dragon wasn't there.

"No," he said eventually. "No, thanks."

Albie turned, trying not to cry,
and ran back up the hill.

Later, Albie's heart still felt STING-Y and CROSS. He sat hugging his knees for a while, until he heard someone drawing near.

It was the girl who was always reading by herself.

She sat down nearby,
opened her book and
read quietly for a little
while . . .

before leaning over, reaching out her hand . . .

and tickling the dragon's nose!

Albie's eyes widened as the
FRIEND DRAGON nuzzled the
girl's cheek and wrapped its
wings gently round them both.

That night, Albie sat thinking
as he ate his supper.

"Perhaps . . ." he said, watching his mother
make some tea. "Perhaps I will have
someone over to play after all."

Mum studied his
face a moment.
"OK," she said,
ruffling his hair.

The night before his new friend came
to play, Albie dreamed a beautiful dragon.
A WIND DRAGON that blustered and blew
and whistled. It would shift colour from blue
to white to a stormy grey.

Albie and his mum watched the WIND DRAGON playing in the garden among the first flowers of spring as they waited for the doorbell to ring.

And then
suddenly . . .

"Come on!"
he shouted to the dragon.
"Iris is here!"

Albie ran to the door to open it, and when he did,

he saw something quite impossible . . .

A TIGER!

Huge and furry, its enormous paws padded and soft,
and behind it was Iris. She smiled shyly at Albie.

"I hope you don't mind . . ."
she said softly.

"You see, I dream tigers."

Albie's heart sang as he watched the
dragon and the tiger bow to each other.

And so Albie and Iris
became the best of FRIENDS . . .

and together they created worlds . . .

more beautiful than either of them
could have imagined alone.

And whatever they did,
and wherever they went,

their DRAGONS
and TIGERS
and DREAMS
always followed.

For Hedd, Gwenno and Guto. Never pretend your dragons aren't there – C.L.

To Angel, for being my support – C.S.

PUFFIN BOOKS

UK | USA | Canada | Ireland | Australia | India | New Zealand | South Africa

Puffin Books is part of the Penguin Random House group of companies
whose addresses can be found at global.penguinrandomhouse.com.

www.penguin.co.uk   www.puffin.co.uk   www.ladybird.co.uk

Penguin
Random House
UK

First published 2022
001

Text copyright © Caryl Lewis, 2022
Illustrations copyright © Carmen Saldaña, 2022
The moral right of the author and illustrator has been asserted

Printed in China

The authorized representative in the EEA is Penguin Random House Ireland,
Morrison Chambers, 32 Nassau Street, Dublin D02 YH68

A CIP catalogue record for this book is available from the British Library

ISBN: 978–0–241–48981–9

All correspondence to: Puffin Books, Penguin Random House Children's,
One Embassy Gardens, 8 Viaduct Gardens, London SW11 7BW